Prince

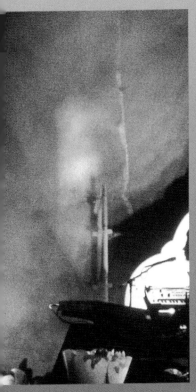

Prince

by Jon Ewing

ORION

AN ORION PAPERBACK

This is a Carlton Book
First published in Great Britain in 1994 by Orion Books Ltd,
Orion House, 5 Upper St Martin's Lane, London WC2H 9EA

Text and design copyright © 1994 Carlton Books Limited
CD Guide format copyright © 1994 Carlton Books Limited

A CIP catalogue record for this book is available from the British Library.
ISBN 1 85797 899 4

Edited, designed and typeset by Haldane Mason
Printed in Italy

The author
Jon Ewing is a freelance journalist, who writes regularly for music, film and computer games magazines.
The author would like to thank David Woolf from Poole-Edwards, Andrew Kenny at WEA,
and Eileen Murton at Controversy.

Picture Acknowledgements
Photographs reproduced by kind permission of **London Features International**; **Pictorial Press**/George Chin, /Larry Kaplan,
/Terry McGough, /Natkin, /Star File; **Redferns** /Richie Aaron; **Retna Pictures** /Mark Anderson, /Larry Busacca, /Gary Gershoff,
/Niels Van Iperen; **Rex Features** /Crollalanza, /Clive Dixon, /Emerson, /John Gooch, /Lenquette, /Rex USA, /SIPA;
Syndicated International Network /David Anderson, /Jana, /Virginia Turbett. Front cover picture **Pictorial Press**.

Contents

Introduction

The diminutive Prince Roger Nelson is a giant among megastars. He has toyed with stardom, mastered it and moved on. From humble beginnings he has risen through the music business by virtue of talent and sheer hard work. In 15 years he has released 15 albums, working at a rate that would put many in an early grave. He is often compared to Michael Jackson, and indeed the similarities are striking: the two artists are the same age, both black, both from musical families, and both breathtaking dancers. Each has become a phenomenal success by uniting white and black fans and bringing dance music to a huge popular audience. And, sadly, both Jackson and Prince have retreated into self-imposed seclusion to avoid the relentless scrutiny of the public eye.

However, the two stars also differ crucially. Michael Jackson's 20-year solo career has produced only a handful of albums, while Prince's songwriting is so prolific that his studio vaults hold three times the number of recordings featured on his first 15 albums. On a whim he created funk band The Time, and almost saw their popularity eclipse his own. His incognito work has often made stars of his peers and collaborators; in 1990, when his own career moved awkwardly through a period of change, a forgotten Prince song called 'Nothing Compares 2 U' became one of the year's most-played singles, crowning the then unknown Sinead O'Connor with sudden international fame.

More than just a unique singer, Prince is also a virtuoso musician, writer, dancer and impresario. Often described as a genius, his presence is an inspiration, his sex-appeal notoriously magnetic. Most radically of all, having risen from the obscurity of the black R&B scene to become a household name, Prince has now dared to throw away the very name itself.

Chapter 1

Boy Genius

Although it might suit the story, it would be an exaggeration to say that Prince Roger Nelson was an extraordinary child. Like most, he had his moments of glory at school, but for most of his youth he blended into the background, only occasionally showing the potential for flamboyancy that, years later, would make him the focus of millions of teenage dreams.

The twin cities
Mattie Shaw first met John L. Nelson when she began singing with a trio

Boy Genius

called the Prince Rogers Band, in which John was the cool-tempered pianist. Their first child was born on June 7, 1958, shortly after their marriage, and they named him Prince Roger after the group that had brought them together. They lived on the north side of Minneapolis, in the state of Minnesota on the USA's cold northern rim. The twin cities of Minneapolis and St Paul were home to around two million people, less than 5 per cent of them black. It is a predominantly industrial area, and although John Nelson lived for his music, he made the bulk of his income as a plastics moulder with the huge electronics company Honeywell Computers.

John and Mattie were two very different personalities who for a short time thrived on the friction between them. However, Prince and his sister, Tika Evene (born in 1960), were to witness the break-up of their parents' marriage in 1965. The semi-autobiographical movie *Purple Rain* might be taken as a suggestion of the importance of that time in Prince's life. The story's nameless hero escapes from the paradoxical extremes of his parents' relationship into a life that is dominated by sexual experimentation and dynamic musical performance. The ambitions of "The Kid"

Opposite page: *Prince's father and date at the Spago restaurant in Hollywood, in October 1986.*

"He's a mentally disturbed young man," said Rick James, with whom Prince toured in 1980. *"What worries me is that so many people relate to him as a representative of black America. He doesn't even want to be black."*

9

closely mirror Prince's own reputation, and it seems a fair assumption that the film is in some way an exorcism of that painful experience.

However, the break-up of his family did not leave the boy in despair. Using the piano that his father had left behind, Prince taught himself to play the theme tunes to favourite TV shows like *The Munsters* and *Batman*, and managed to master the instrument by the age of ten, almost despite the efforts of his music tutor at John Hay Elementary. As his home life deteriorated (his mother was forced to take on three jobs to support them, leaving her little time for her children), Prince retreated further into his music. Mattie remarried in 1967, but Prince could not stand to live in the same house as his stepfather. He ran away from home for the first time in 1970. For a couple of years, he was shuttled from one unsatisfactory home to another. He lived briefly with his father, who bought him his first guitar and taught him to play. He moved on to an aunt named Olivia, but her preaching and his guitar made bad company, and he

was finally taken in by the family of his schoolfriend André Anderson in 1972. The two teenagers used the family basement to rehearse, and in 1974 they formed their first band: Grand Central.

Early learning

The Anderson household has been described as Prince's second family, his private sanctuary for musical exploration and a hotbed of sexual awakening. It is likely that the more extraordinary of the stories that André and Prince have told about that time (all-night orgies sanctioned by André's mother, for example) were exaggerations, but there is no doubt that these were the years that saw Prince's future take shape.

Grand Central had a friendly rivalry with a local high-school band called Flyte Tyme, which was fronted for a while by Alexander O'Neal. Both bands played cover versions by Top 40 artists like Carol King, Sly Stone and Grover Washington, and performed in back yards around the neighbourhood, at the YMCA, or at school discos.

Prince on stage with the first of his several bands, Grand Central.

As a "white" state, the region's access to "black" music came mainly from the chart success of Motown artistes such as Stevie Wonder. Prince was as much exposed to Joni Mitchell and Santana as to any black culture, and the nightlife and radio stations of the city catered for, at best, a

"I wrote like I was rich,
like I had been everywhere
and seen everything
and been with every woman
in the world."

Prince

mixed audience. The Andersons' basement became a focal point for 20 or more friends and relations who loved to play music together and had nowhere else to go.

As a practising Seventh Day Adventist, Prince had attended church every Sunday, but for years he was too shy to sing, except in the privacy of his own room. As the Seventies progressed, however, he became more expert as a musician. At first he was just part of a mainly instrumental group, but as he and

André both learned to play bass guitar, drums and saxophone, he began to dictate the arrangements to the rest of the band. As they incorporated new chart hits into their set, Prince found himself teaching the other band members to play their parts, and before long he became the group's frontman.

Moon Sound

In 1976 the band (who had changed their name to Champagne in deference to Graham Central Station, a funk band formed by ex-Family Stone multi-instrumentalist Larry Graham), booked some time at a small studio called Moon Sound. The owner was Chris Moon, an advertising executive

Chris Moon had to help Prince to overcome his initial shyness by suggesting he lie on the floor of the studio in the dark to record his first vocal tracks.

From the very start, Prince's songs took place in a bedroom of the mind. In time, he made the stage into nothing more than an extension of his boudoir.

who dabbled in writing and recording. In the hope of developing a writing partnership with Prince, he offered the boy the keys to the studio so that he could begin to learn the principles of sound recording each day after school.

Chris Moon advised the teenager to drop his band (with the exception of André Anderson) and even his surname, to which Prince reluctantly agreed. Together they wrote 'Soft And Wet', a bouncy disco number that was to become Prince's first single. Like the other tracks recorded at Moon Sound, it was a long and overblown version of the song. As Prince later recalled, "I wrote like I was rich, like I had been everywhere and seen everything and been with every woman in the world." He revealed his obsession through the notorious song 'Machine' (never released), which likened the individual parts of the female anatomy to the workings of an engine.

American Artists Inc.
Prince graduated from Central High School on his eighteenth birthday

and immediately headed for New York. He stayed with his half-sister Sharon while he took his four-track demo —'Baby', 'Machine', 'Soft And Wet' and 'My Love Is Forever'— round the record companies. Sharon showed some interest in representing Prince herself, and arranged an audition, at which Prince suffered the gruelling experience of singing one of his songs unaccompanied while French producer Danielle Mauroy looked on. However, her offer of a publishing deal was to seem laughable in comparison to the enormous record deal waiting just around the corner, for back in Minneapolis Chris Moon was making progress. He took a copy of Prince's demo to fellow advertising executive Owen Husney, who also moonlighted in the music business. Husney was very impressed by the songs and even more impressed by the singer. He called for the pop primadonna to return to his home town and in September 1976 formed the impressive-sounding management company American Artists Inc. with Prince as his first signing.

Husney wasted no time in capitalizing on his young singer's potential. He raised about $50,000 (£33,300) to promote Prince as professionally as he could, hiring out the top local 24-track studio Sound 80 and commissioning several glossy promo packs. Taking the sparkling new demo tapes, he set off for Los Angeles in March 1977.

In business

American Artists Inc. was offered contracts by CBS, Warner Brothers and A&M Records, although all were dubious about Prince's determination to produce his début album himself. Eventually, Warners gave in. One apocryphal story tells how three big-name producers were hired by Warners to dress as janitors and covertly assess Prince's competence as he worked alone in the studio. Other reports suggest that he was openly auditioned in front of studio representatives. Whatever the truth, the result was success: Prince was signed up with an extremely generous six-figure contract on June 25, 1977.

Prince was often frustrated by his deep voice, saying he "couldn't get any life from it".

17

Owen Husney and his wife Britt left Minneapolis and rented a house north of San Francisco, so that Prince could work at the famous Record Plant in Sausolito, where both Sly Stone and Carlos Santana had previously recorded. With the "help" of executive producer Tommy Vicari—whose presence Prince resented but was forced to endure—the début album *For You* was made, which was released on April 7, 1978.

Prince worked for 12 hours a day over five months to create *For You*, and, not surprisingly, it lacks the spontaneity of his later records. He insisted on absolute perfection and the recording is flawless, but it is precisely this workmanlike feel that dampens the album's vitality. The first track, 'For You', heralds Prince's penchant for a dramatic opening. Its multi-layered a cappella harmonies evoke the sound of a large church choir, echoed on the front cover, which features a blurred photograph of Prince looking like a doe-eyed choirboy with an enormous Afro haircut. However, the reverse side of the cover shows a very different Prince, perched cross-legged and naked on a couch, holding an acoustic guitar as he seemingly drifts through outer space.

If *For You* has any significance in Prince's career, it is in the dual nature of the cover: on the one hand the shy, dedicated boy, and on the other a sexy and enigmatic New Age star.

The first Prince single, 'Soft And Wet', released in June 1978 as Prince turned 20, was a forgettable pop

*Sitting on the edge
of the stage for
'Blues In C (If I
Had A Harem)'.*

tune, but it was surprisingly successful. A promotional tour of the States created quite a stir, and at one record-signing session in North Carolina, 3,000 fans reportedly came to see the boy genius.

So near and yet so far

Warner Brothers wanted to see Prince on tour as soon as possible, and he returned to Minneapolis to put a band together. His oldest friend, André Anderson, was the obvious choice to play bass, and André took his middle name, Simon, to become André Cymone on stage. An equally obvious choice as drummer was Prince's cousin Chazz Smith, a familiar face from the Anderson house. However, determined to form a multi-racial band, Prince instead offered the drumming stool to Owen Husney's gofer Bobby Rivkin, who was known as Bobby Z. Dez Dickerson, a black glam-rock guitarist, was hired via a newspaper advert, and two white musicians, Matt Fink and Gayle Chapman, came in as keyboard players.

By the end of 1978, with the failure of the single 'Just As Long As We're Together', Prince felt that his career was unlikely to advance without new management. He asked Linster "Pepe" Willie, a Brooklyn musician married to Prince's cousin, to promote two showcase concerts for him at the Capri Theatre in Minneapolis in January 1979. The band rehearsed tirelessly, but Prince was not quite ready for fame. "I find it extremely hard to perform for people," he confessed to the *Minneapolis Tribune*. The VIPs from Warner Brothers, who had flown in from the West Coast, were very disappointed by Prince's lack of star quality. Any thoughts of a tour were shelved and Prince went back to the drawing board.

Pepe Willie had big plans, but not the talent to make them work. His only contribution to Prince's career was the 1985 release of an uninspired

album, *The Minneapolis Genius: 94 East, The Historic 1977 Recordings*— having often sat in on Champagne sessions, Willie had asked Prince and André to play with his own band, 94 East. Most of the tracks,

Prince recorded early versions of 'Soft And Wet' and 'My Love Is Forever' at his Moon Sound sessions in 1976.

During the 1977 Minneapolis Genius sessions with Pepe Willie, Prince worked on early demos of 'I Feel For You' and 'Do Me Baby'.

unfortunately, are incomplete, as the album is almost wholly instrumental. The deal Pepe made with Polydor fell through just as Prince's career began to take off, and the *Historic* tapes are incidental to the big picture.

"I wanted a hit album. It was for the radio rather than me, but it got a lot of people interested in my music."

Prince

The first hit

In June 1979 Prince arrived at Alpha Studios in Burbank, California, where it took him only six weeks to record his second album, *Prince*. Since January he had written more than 20 songs, including an early version of 'Purple Rain'. The nine-track album was a huge improvement on Prince's first outing, and the quality translated directly into record sales. At the end of August 'I Wanna Be Your Lover' was released as a single

and became his first hit. With its breathy, high-pitched vocal and provocative lyrics, it stayed just the right side of wholesome entertainment to gain significant radio play, reaching Number 1 on the black chart and Number 11 on the national chart. Later that year it became his first UK single, reaching Number 41. 'I Wanna Be Your Lover' was to sell more than a million copies.

Prince later claimed that the album was "contrived". "I wanted a hit album," he said. "It was for the radio rather than me, but it got a lot of people interested in my music." Consequently, hooks and melodies replaced the verbose instrumentation of *For You*, and the lyrics were less sexually explicit. With heavy use of the synthesizer to provide the light and catchy tunes behind 'I Feel For You'

(later a massive hit for Chaka Khan in 1984) and 'Why You Wanna Treat Me So Bad?' (a minor hit single in January 1980), Prince had reinvented himself as a pop product, though he claimed, casually, "I don't think about success—it's all just part of

"I don't think about success—it's all just part of the Dream Factory. If it happens, it happens."
Prince, February 1980

the Dream Factory. If it happens, it happens."

Sexy dancer
The auditorium was, sadly, only half full when Prince returned to Minneapolis on February 9, 1980.

However, those who did turn up to the Orpheum Theatre were galvanized by Prince's shocking new look and the hard, funk-rock sound. The show was far more daring and crude than the glossy pop sound of *Prince*. As part of the band's new image, Prince had combed down his Afro and wore zebra-striped bikini briefs, high-heeled boots and legwarmers. Matt Fink wore a surgeon's costume, including stethoscope and rubber gloves, and took on the stage name "Doctor" Fink.

Although Prince had been known chiefly as a fresh, talented multi-instrumentalist, his promiscuity soon became the media talking point. The *Soho Daily News* in New York noted "Prince necking on the platform with his sexy blonde keyboardist", and Prince invariably was seen "humping" his microphone stand or his guitar. Suddenly he was more famous for his underwear than for his music—and he preferred it that way.

The "Battle of Funk" tour
Through the spring and summer of 1980 *Prince* sold steadily, although a third single, 'Still Waiting', did

nothing. Warners arranged a two-month tour with Prince as support to glam funk star Rick James. The media and promoters tried to instil a sense of rivalry between them—Prince the young pretender and James the coarse, raunchy funk star—and it is likely that there was little love lost between the two. James described

Prince with Dez Dickerson (above) and with André Cymone (left), a Grand Central original who didn't survive long in the shadow of Prince's personality.

Prince learned to play guitar with his friend André Anderson in the basement of André's house.

Prince in the UK magazine *Blues & Soul* as "a little science fiction creep" and Prince spent most of the tour trying to upstage him. But much of the rivalry can realistically be put down to PR rumour-mongering aimed at getting press coverage.

Spaghetti Inc.

Since parting company with manager Owen Husney at the end of 1978, Prince had looked at several potential replacements, but found no one with the right feel for his music. In 1979 he finally settled on Spaghetti Inc., an LA management company owned by music business stalwarts Bob Cavallo and Joe Ruffalo. From then on, Prince came under the wing of personal manager Steve Fargnoli.

Meanwhile Gayle Chapman was unhappy with Prince's radical new direction. Songs like 'Head', previewed on the Rick James tour, are said to have clashed irreconcilably with her religious beliefs, and she left to be replaced on keyboards by Lisa Coleman. Prince's new material was as strongly sexual as his costumes. Dez Dickerson's on-stage guitar pyrotechnics provided the rock power, but he too was unsure about the new direction. "I divorced myself from the costume side of it," he said later. "I thought if he wants to go out in a gerbil suit, fine, do it. But I began to feel sex had been overdone in rock'n'roll."

Prince and manager Steve Fargnoli share some quality time on the Lovesexy '88 tour bus.

Chapter 2

Controversy

On October 8, 1980, aged just 22, Prince released his third solo album, *Dirty Mind,* in the US. He had spent that summer alone in his Minneapolis home, recording in his own 16-track basement studio, and had originally intended the tracks to be demo versions. However, Steve Fargnoli convinced him that the raw rocking of the eight songs was a perfect follow-up to the polished pop sound of *Prince*. It marked a turning point in the singer's career.

The album was not to be a chart success, but it began Prince's journey out of the R&B chart ghetto into worldwide acceptance as a rock singer. Its rock slant was evident on the chugging riff of the title track and the vicious metal guitar solo on 'Sister'. It was almost universally lauded, although the strong sexual overtones caused problems with radio stations. On 'Head' Prince sang explicitly about oral sex, while 'Sister' dealt with the temptations of incest. As a consequence, *Dirty Mind*

Controversy

represented a massive leap forward in Prince's quest for world domination, but half a step back in record sales. While *Prince* had sold almost a million copies, *Dirty Mind* did not reach the 500,000 mark until the release of *Purple Rain* boosted his back catalogue in 1984.

The birth of a band

Prince spent the autumn in Minneapolis putting together a new band called The Time. His old friend and ex-Grand Central drummer Morris Day was to be the frontman, with former Flyte Tyme members Terry Lewis (bass), Monte Moir and Jimmy Jam Harris (both on keys), and Jellybean Johnson (drums) along with promising young virtuoso guitarist Jesse Johnson. Prince created the band from scratch, and his motives for doing so at such a crucial point in his career are still uncertain. One story suggests that Morris Day allowed Prince to take credit for one of his songs—'Uptown'—and in return, Prince promised to get him a record deal. At any rate, most

Semi-naked ambition: Prince in 1980.

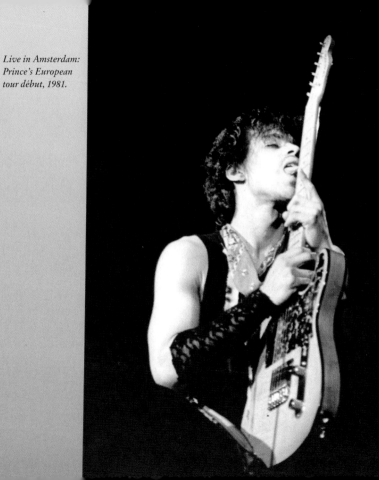

*Live in Amsterdam:
Prince's European
tour début, 1981.*

sources now agree that he actually played most of the instruments on The Time's albums, although no one realized this until a sharp journalist put two and two together in 1981. The sound of The Time was what Morris Day described as "funk and roll", but their image was all-important to their

"I'm really shy when I meet someone for the first time. I'm supposed to be a mysterious person, but I'm not mysterious."

Prince

success—the band dressed cool and acted macho, and Prince gave them slick, funky pop songs to match.

Baby, I'm a star

Throughout December 1980 Prince toured the small theatres and clubs of America, playing an 11-song set that lasted less than an hour. The shows were tight and professional, with the

flamboyant Prince dressed in his now-famous trenchcoat and bikini briefs. The audience were still predominantly adult and black, but the tide was beginning to turn. Bill Adler was moved to describe Prince in a *Rolling Stone* review as "a star", and when the young singer went on to almost sell out the 12,000-seat Cobo

"To me it's one of the largest compliments I could pay a woman, to say that I like how you look in fishnet pantyhose."
—Morris Day

Eight hundred and ninety people saw Prince at the Paradiso Club in Amsterdam in May 1981.

Arena in Detroit, the proof seemed to be there in the ticket sales.

An interview in the *LA Times* just before Christmas revealed the reason for Prince's media reclusiveness in later years: "I'm really shy when I meet someone for the first time," he said. "I'm supposed to be a mysterious person, but I'm not mysterious." Although that statement seems hard to reconcile with the shroud of enigma that covers Prince today, it is interesting to note that most of the interviews he has given in his 16-year career date from around that time. Publicist Howard Bloom had been hired by Steve Fargnoli in New York to capitalize on Prince's "crossover" potential—industry jargon for a sound that could be marketed to black (funk) as well as white (rock) record buyers. Grudgingly, Prince agreed to a series of telephone interviews. The telephone gave him a distance he needed, but he was clearly uncomfortable when asked any personal questions. Chris Callis, who photographed Prince in 1978 and

32

1979, only remembers that "he just didn't talk".

Prince's first full feature in *Rolling Stone* in February 1981 predicted his universal success, but at the time the exposure had little impact on record sales—which may have led Prince to believe that gruelling interviews were a waste of time.

Across the Atlantic

'Dirty Mind', released as a single in the US in November, had been a

"From the moment the dirty-macked and minded frontline of Prince, Dez and Andre twirled around to face the crowd, the whole set-up just oozed star impact"—

Betty Page, on Prince's first ever U.K. gig (Sounds, June 1981)

failure. 'Do It All Night' and the *Dirty Mind* album out-take 'Gotta Stop (Messin' About)' were both released as singles in the UK, but did not chart despite extensive advertising and a brief European tour. Prince's trip to the UK had long been awaited by the press, who were thrilled by reports of his dynamic appearance on stage. His first visit across the Atlantic in May, taking in Amsterdam, London and Paris respectively, blew away the audiences, and he was interviewed in the three major UK music papers

"With a dash of kohl black to accentuate what is at once a heavy stare and a prissy one, he actually looks rather untidy: not so much a style guerilla as an uptight eight-year-old in fancy dress."
—Dave Hill, Prince, a Pop Life.

Controversy

of the time, *Melody Maker*, *Sounds* and *NME*. In *Sounds*, Betty Page described the impact of Prince's first UK concert in June: "From the moment the dirty-macked and minded frontline of Prince, Dez and André twirled around to face the crowd, the whole set-up just oozed star impact."

Typically, Prince did not take a break before returning to the USA to work on his fourth album in Minneapolis and LA. Meanwhile The Time released their own eponymous début album, and the band's up-tempo dance melodies were a great success, garnering two Top 10 hits in the black chart. In fact, the album sold more copies than *Dirty Mind*.

At that time, Prince's long-time collaborator André Cymone decided to quit Prince's band to pursue a solo career. The relationship between the two friends had been sorely tried over the past three years, and André rightly believed that he had little opportunity for success in his own right while he remained in Prince's shadow. His bass-playing shoes were

filled by 18-year-old Mark Brown, more commonly known as Brown Mark, who was already a minor Minneapolis celebrity.

1982: Touring with his fourth album, Controversy.

Left to right: *Susan Moonsi, Denise Matthews* and *Brenda Bennett— collectively known as Vanity 6.*

raunchy rock 'n' roll guitar licks, the two LA shows were disastrous. The crowd were restless and abusive, and although the band eventually decided to grit their teeth and return to the stage on the second day, they survived the insults of the audience for only three songs.

Controversy

Three days later, on October 14, 1981, Prince's fourth album was released under the title *Controversy*. The title track had failed to make an impact as a single a few weeks earlier, and some journalists were already predicting that his day might have come and gone. Prince did no interviews and was forced to suffer some very mixed reviews from the critics, yet the album was a big success, reaching Number 21 and remaining in the US charts for 63 weeks in all.

Controversy provoked less of a storm over lyrical content, if only because the pundits had learned what to expect from a new Prince record. Four of the songs, 'Let's Work', 'Do Me Baby', 'Private Joy' and 'Jack U Off' were overtly sexual. 'Ronnie

Can't get no satisfaction

Debuting his new material at two astounding gigs at local hideaway Sam's, Prince prepared for success with a finished album in October. However, past comparisons with the strutting Mick Jagger were brought into sharp contrast when he and his band were given a minor support slot with the Rolling Stones at the vast 100,000 capacity Memorial Coliseum in Los Angeles. Despite Prince's attempts to wow the crowd with

Controversy

Talk To Russia', on the other hand, was a numbingly conformist political plea and 'Annie Christian' was a bewildering song about gun control and irreligious wickedness, far too inscrutable to cause any offence. Musically the album was a natural progression from the last, but it did not have a sufficiently universal appeal to change his career. That was to come less than a year later.

The following month, with The Time in support, the Controversy tour began in Pittsburgh with a more sophisticated show, as Prince abandoned the trenchcoat and briefs in favour of black trousers, white shirt and bow tie. Setting the tone for future extravagant shows, the stage had two tiers with ramps, fire poles and billowing, purple-lit smoke. Prince performed for up to 85 minutes every night, seducing the audience into a fever and exploding into encores of 'Jack U Off' and 'Sexuality'. He ended the show with a scene of mock crucifixion, unmasking the religious-sexual overtones he was to stress later in his career. "I think my problem is that

"I think my problem is that my attitude's so sexual that it overshadows everything else."

Prince

my attitude's so sexual that it overshadows everything else," he said.

The outrageous and under-dressed Vanity 6: the perfect complement to Prince's own flamboyant performances.

Playing and filling venues of up to 8,000 capacity all over the US, Prince was building a reputation as one of the best black live performers in rock history, alongside James Brown and Jimi Hendrix. However, a supposedly triumphant homecoming proved to be another letdown when only 5,580 tickets were sold for a March 7 show at the 13,500-capacity Met Center in Bloomington, Minneapolis.

Sidelines

After the tour Prince began work on three separate projects: a new support act—Vanity 6, an all-girl trio fronted by ex-porn-movie actress Denise Matthews—a second Time album and a fifth solo album.

Working from his own basement studio—now with a far more professional 24 tracks—Prince recorded the eponymous début album for Vanity 6, which went gold (500,000 copies) on its release in the US that summer. With their image of voluptuous, demanding sexuality, the trio were unambiguously provocative and erotic. Appearing in lacy underwear or flimsy, diaphanous clothing, Vanity 6 released four successful singles from the album, including the notorious 'Nasty Girl', which included the lyrics: "I can't control it, I need seven inches or more...Get it up, I can't wait any more."

The Time's second album, *What Time Is It?*, was released two weeks later, and sold even more copies than the first. Featuring the pouting, bouffanted Morris Day surrounded by clocks on the cover, it was a camp and stylized album loaded with catchy pop songs. As with the Vanity records, Prince is given no credit on

Left to right:
*Bobby Z, Wendy
Melvoin and Prince
at the American
Music Awards.*

the sleeve, but copyright in the songs can be traced back to him, and insiders have revealed that he not only produced and wrote the songs, but also played most of the instruments on both *Vanity 6* and *What Time Is It?*

1999

Somehow, in the meantime, Prince had recorded his own new album, a collection of 11 lengthy tracks that branched out further than ever from his black roots. A single called '1999', released in September 1982, made a small splash, reaching Number 44 in the US charts. However, the double album of the same name that followed a month later truly launched Prince irreversibly into the star system. *1999* was a vast and sprawling album and

Controversy

Steve Fargnoli had to fight tooth and claw with Warner Brothers to convince them to release the two-record set in the States. In the UK, where Prince's celebrity was still very minor, a seven-track single-album version was released instead.

Acknowledging his band for the first time, the album was credited to Prince and the Revolution, and featured his two most commercial songs to date, 'Little Red Corvette' and 'Delirious', as well as hardcore, sexual dance grooves like 'DMSR' and 'Lady Cab Driver'. Other notable tracks include 'All The Critics Love U In New York', a candid look into the superlatives of those writers who chose to call him "genius"; 'Free', a beautiful song of thanksgiving that set the standard for the epic sweep of 'Purple Rain'; and the title track, a classic party anthem destined to be filling the dancefloors when the end of the millennium finally comes. The opening verses are distinctive because the lines are shared alternately by Prince, guitarist Dez Dickerson and keyboard-player Lisa Coleman. The recording was originally intended as

a three-part harmony, but it is indicative of Prince's growing inventiveness in the studio that he had the vision to experiment, with memorable results.

Triple threat

After a series of scheduled pre-tour interviews had been cancelled when only the first had taken place, the Triple Threat Tour took to the road in Chattanooga on November 11. The tour was intended to close at the 19,200-seat Reunion Arena in Dallas, Texas on New Year's Eve, but on December 16, one seemingly minor event changed Prince's career and finally exposed him to a huge audience hitherto unaware of his talent. A new 24-hour pop video channel called MTV (Music Television), which already had a 15 million-strong following of mainly white, teenage rock fans, added the video of '1999' to their playlist. The reaction was phenomenal. Prince's popularity went sky high, and the tour went on for a further four months.

The Triple Threat Tour was unmissable. Before Prince took the stage, the audience was given a punchy—albeit rather amateurish—20-minute warm-up from Vanity 6, after which the show continued with a full set by The Time, who had been behind a curtain, playing the instruments for Vanity. The Time were at the peak of their career, not only in terms of record sales, but also as performers. However, band members have claimed that they were paid only $140 (£93) each per week, and during the tour, jealousy began to rear its head. Prince may have perceived The Time as a Frankenstein's monster rising up against its creator—he said, "The Time were, to be perfectly honest, the only band I was afraid of. They were turning into, like, Godzilla."

There was mutiny, too, within Prince's own ranks. Dez Dickerson found it hard to deal with the pressures of success and by his own admission was becoming increasingly difficult to work with. (In an unreleased demo from the period, 'Extra Lovable', Prince sings the teasing line, "Dez, don't you like my band?") Aware of the distance that was growing between Prince and his

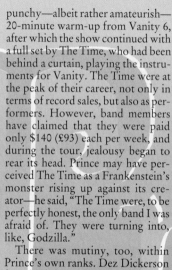

> *"The Time were, to be perfectly honest, the only band I was afraid of. They were turning into, like, Godzilla."*
>
> Prince

old friends, many of the entourage blamed manager Steve Fargnoli for coming between them, as well as a new addition to the team, the giant bodyguard Chick Huntsberry, who was notoriously over-protective and impassable.

All the Critics Love U
While tempers seethed backstage, in public Prince was master of all he surveyed. The set opened with him silhouetted against a bright light that was masked by blinds as he sang 'Controversy', sliding down to stage level on a fireman's pole to launch into 'Let's Work'. He now put as much emphasis on light-footed choreography as he did on costume, and his

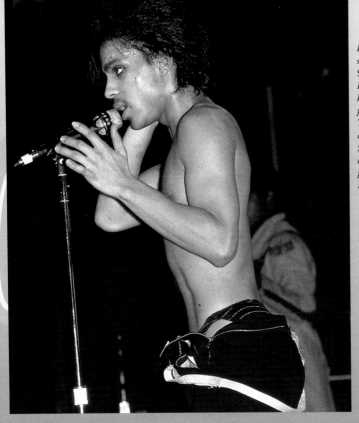

In 1983 Prince snubbed Rolling Stone *magazine's Debby Miller when he failed to give a promised interview. The publishers had commissioned a $10,000 (£6,700) cover shoot by photographer Richard Avedon.*

45

Lisa Coleman (left) *became Prince's keyboard player in 1980. Her friend Wendy Melvoin* (right) *joined up on guitar in 1983.*

reputation as a dancer began to be the envy of even Michael Jackson. The tour was a huge success, using the same extravagant stage set as before, this time including a brass bed that rose up in front of the blinds at the top of the stage at the finale of the show. Thrashing and moaning on the bed in mock ecstasy, Prince sang 'International Lover' as he stripped off his clothing before doing a rousing encore of '1999'.

'Little Red Corvette' was the first single to seal Prince's pop fame, reaching Number 6 in the US charts in February 1983. In the UK his statistics were less convincing; the only UK hit single he had scored in over three years was '1999', which reached Number 25. As a consequence, two London gigs scheduled for January (Hammersmith Odeon, now the Labatts Apollo) and April (the Dominion Theatre) were both cancelled without explanation. In the United States the venues had grown to capacities of up to 20,000, including a sell-out return show at the Met Center in Bloomington, after which all the members of the tour played a brief late-night jam session at an exclusive party at the local Registry Hotel. The tour ended in Chicago in April, having grossed a colossal $10 million (£6.6 million), making Prince one of the most successful touring artists of 1983.

Controversy

However, the end of the tour saw the departure of Dez Dickerson for an uneventful solo career. He was replaced on guitar by Lisa Coleman's old schoolfriend Wendy Melvoin.

Purple prose

Throughout the tour Prince had been writing notes in a small purple book, and during the spring of 1983 he and screenwriter William Blinn began to work out a script for a movie to be called *Dreams*. They shuttled changes to the script backwards and forwards until the tour was over, by which time the skeletal structure of a movie was in place. Prince told Blinn that he wanted the word "purple" to be in the title, and the result was *Purple Rain*.

Chapter 3

The Purple Prince

As Prince's contract with Cavallo and Ruffalo came to an end in 1983, Steve Fargnoli worked day and night to see that the deal was renewed. The world's hottest new pop star wanted only one thing that year: to be a movie star. It might have seemed an impossible dream, but somehow Fargnoli persuaded Warner Brothers to put up $4 million (£2.6 million) for *Purple Rain*.

The Number 6 hit 'Little Red Corvette' was followed up by another Top 10 hit, 'Delirious', in August, but international success was still evading Prince, if only through lack of touring outside the USA. 'Little Red Corvette' was released twice in Britain in 1983, with two different B-sides, and it flopped both times. So *Purple Rain* was an opportunity to break Prince into new territories abroad, and Warner Brothers' relatively small investment paid off in spades.

Moving picture

According to William Blinn, the original script of *Purple Rain* was a dark, brooding tale in which The Kid (played by Prince) would have been torn between life (represented by explicit sex scenes and explosive live performances) and death (as his father murders his mother before turning the gun on himself). However, after Blinn left to work on a third series of *Fame* for TV, the project fell into the hands of Albert Magnoli, whose student short *Jazz* had been showered with praise. Unfortunately, Magnoli's vision of Prince's semi-autobiographical story was more pat, and the sex and violence was demoted to a sub-plot in favour of a light-hearted yarn involving the rivalry between

The Kid's band and Morris Day's The Time.

In the event, it is Day who steals the scene in acting terms. His extraordinary, overblown costumes and jive-talking patois with his sidekick Jerome Benton (especially their choice pastiche of the classic Abbott and Costello sketch "Who's On First?" puts Prince's stone-faced character in the shade. Day became quite a fixture on TV chat shows

Jerome Benton and Morris Day in Purple Rain.

Patricia Kotero was chosen from 700 hopefuls to become "Apollonia".

when the movie was released, and carried off his sharp-suited lounge-lizard character nicely into real life. Were it not for a debilitating cocaine addiction, he might have eclipsed Prince's movie career altogether.

One team member who did not take part was Denise Matthews. At the eleventh hour she announced that she was leaving the movie and Vanity 6 to try a solo career. Rumours of sexual or financial disputes between Prince and Vanity cannot be proved one way or the other. One story suggests that their entire relationship was just one of Prince's devious plans to embarrass Rick James, who had been involved with Denise when Prince first met her.

After a frantic search involving 700 auditions, Vanity's part was given to 22-year-old model Patricia Kotero, who Prince renamed Apollonia, after a character in *The Godfather*. She became the leader of Apollonia 6, which was destined to become one of his least inspired collaborations, as well as

"I always tease him that he's a verbally conservative gentleman. Because he is. But when you see him, even in his kitchen, he is still bigger than life."

Apollonia (aka Patricia Kotero) 1984

Prince

The Purple Prince

taking on the role of Prince's love interest in *Purple Rain*. The movie was shot in 32 locations around Minneapolis, and the live scenes took place at the Union Bar in Old St Anthony and First Avenue (formerly Sam's), which subsequently became a sacred shrine for Prince's pilgrims.

"Everything Prince did from the beginning was a plan. We just watched it all happen like he said it would."

Jimmy Jam Harris (The Time)

During post-production of the movie in early 1984, Prince gave The Time a little space to record their third album, *Ice Cream Castle*. However, three of the original members—Jimmy Jam, Terry Lewis and Monte Moir—had departed, and the album (released in July 1984) was their least exciting. Prince's influence on the band was still sufficiently oppressive that both vocalist Morris Day and guitarist Jesse Johnson decided that they too should pursue solo careers, and by the time the album came out, the band had already split.

Meanwhile, Prince's attention was captured by percussionist Sheila Escovedo. Sheila E, as she was known, was the daughter of Santana drummer

Denise Matthews gave up her place in Vanity 6 and Purple Rain *to pursue a solo career—a departure that was subject to much rumour.*

Peter Escovedo and had performed as a session musician with stars like Diana Ross and Marvin Gaye. Sheila E and Prince admired each other's work, and together they recorded the hard-hitting dance track 'Erotic City'. Prince persuaded Sheila to put together an entire album in just five days, and within weeks not only was she signed up with Cavallo and Ruffalo but she also had her own record deal with Warner Brothers.

Live at the second of six sold-out shows at the Inglewood Forum, Los Angeles, February 19, 1985.

Recorded during the movie's post-production at LA's Sunset Sound, 'When Doves Cry' was released in the US in May 1984. It became Prince's first Number 1 single—which was achievement enough—and remained in the US top spot for six weeks, selling more than two million copies in America alone—the biggest-selling song of the year. It even (finally!) broke the Top 10 in Britain, peaking at Number 4. The surprise hit was full of latent sexuality and despair, with its focus on "the heat between me and you" as the singer's uncharacteristically deep voice described the intense yearning of two star-crossed lovers.

Also that month, and for the second year running, Prince was highly honoured at the Minnesota Music Awards, and took the opportunity to reveal his new image. With his Sergeant Pepper look, in paisley suit and ruffled shirt with Edwardian lace cuffs, he suddenly became the Purple Prince, His Purple Highness, His Royal Purpleness... the media caught on to the colourful motif with gusto.

The Purple Prince

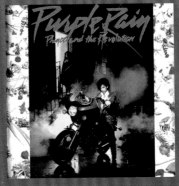

Ostensibly an "official soundtrack" album of the movie, *Purple Rain* featured none of the performances by Apollonia 6 or The Time. But it did for once allow some input from the members of The Revolution, and only three tracks (recorded at Sunset) were credited to Prince alone.

Purple Rain outsold all of his previous albums dramatically, shifting more than a million units in the first week alone, and eventually reaching

"My name is Prince, and I have come to play with you."

an unprecedented 15 million sales worldwide. Musically the album was captivating and wholly original, incorporating elements of Prince's meticulous studio wizardry with reckless, rock 'n' roll abandon. 'The Beautiful Ones' was a Renaissance love song, 'Darling Nikki' was a teasingly lewd metal-funk attack, and 'Baby I'm A Star' was the ultimate in

joyous self-celebration. Yet it was the single material that really took over the airwaves in the summer of 1984. 'When Doves Cry', the rockin' 'Let's Go Crazy' and the pop groove of 'I Would Die 4 U' were irresistible melodies with a hard edge, and truly bridged the gap between black and white audiences. If anything there were more white than black faces in the crowds at this peak in Prince's career, largely thanks to the anthemic 'Purple Rain', which gave even Bruce Springsteen's stadium classic 'Born In The USA' a run for its money.

Opposite page: *The five-month Purple Rain US tour took in more than 100 venues of up to 20,000 capacity.*

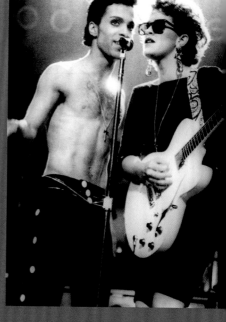

Performing the jangly hit "Kiss" with Wendy in Detroit in 1986; the single reached Number 1 in the US and Number 6 in the UK.

On July 28, 1984, *Purple Rain* opened in 900 cinemas across the United States. After three days the movie had taken $7.8 million (£5.2 million) at the box office, becoming one of the year's biggest successes. It eventually grossed about $70 million (£47 million).

Prince has a well-deserved reputation for performing impromptu concerts to small crowds of adoring fans, and in the warm-up for his forth-coming national tour he made a number of thrilling surprise appearances. Word of mouth alone carried the news of a such gig at First Avenue in Minneapolis, and the police had to be called to turn away more than 2,000 people. In September and October he appeared three times as a guest on Sheila E's tour, and The Revolution popped up under the guise of the mysteriously named Red Hot and Blue at Bogart's in Cincinnati. Meanwhile, 'Let's Go Crazy' became his second Number 1 single in the US, backed with the raunchy Sheila E collaboration, 'Erotic City', which featured the highly controversial chorus: "We can fuck until the dawn, makin' love till cherry's gone." 'Purple Rain' followed closely and went to Number

The Purple Prince

2, featuring the spiritual 'God' on the flipside.

Purple Rain Tour

In November the Purple Rain tour began with seven spectacular sell-out shows at the Joe Louis Arena in Detroit. The Revolution now consisted of Brown Mark (bass), Wendy Melvoin (guitar), Bobby Z (drums) and Lisa Coleman and Matt Fink (keys). Together with Prince they formed a true musical team, and they knocked America on its back with a stunning theatrical show, in which Prince wore more than a dozen costumes as he commanded every inch of the many-layered stage. At the beginning of the performance he would rise from below the stage, showered with petals from above, materializing from a plume of smoke to say "My name is Prince, and I have come to play with you."

Surrounded by lasers, dry ice and hydraulics, Prince performed for up to two hours. Unveiling his trademark custom-made guitars with their beautiful curled headstocks and colour-coordinated paintwork,

he mostly gave the audiences vital, raucous material from the *1999* and *Purple Rain* albums, but also some delicate solo ballads at his purple grand piano. The show would close

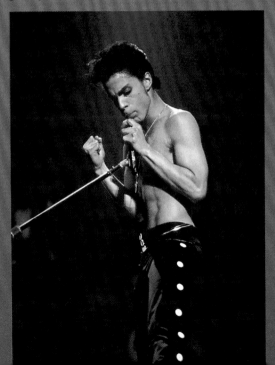

Touring America with Purple Rain. *The audiences loved him, but he was not about to give them* Purple Rain 2.

with a lengthy version of 'Purple Rain' (during which The Revolution were joined on stage by Apollonia, Sheila E and even members of the audience) which left the crowd awe-struck and greedy for more.

The Press bites back

The tour was a colossal financial success, drawing audiences of more than 1.6 million people and grossing $30 million (£20 million). To give a little back to the communities he visited, Prince staged several free performances for handicapped children, and matinée shows for the deaf, at which translators in purple T-shirts interpreted Prince's lyrics (leaving out the more colourful language!). At every concert 'Purple Circle' seats were set aside at $50 (£33) each to raise money for charity, and at his homecoming shows, many tickets were given free to underprivileged youths. Yet despite the warmth of Prince's heart, many journalists were determined to find fault.

Following the American Music Awards in January, where Prince was honoured in three categories, dozens of artists (among them Bruce Springsteen, Bob Dylan and Diana Ross) went to a nearby studio to record a benefit song for Ethiopia—Michael Jackson's 'We Are The World'. Prince chose not to take part, and instead donated a ballad called '4 The Tears In Your Eyes', to be exclusively released on the *USA For Africa* album. The press chose to

"He cannot see us. He sees only the great mirror in his mind's eye, which shows him only his big, royal self."

Richard Grabel, NME

misinterpret the story, and readers were led to believe that Prince had snubbed the other artists involved.

In truth, Prince had become a different—and perhaps less dangerous—kind of star. By the end of the tour The Revolution were burning through the *Billboard* charts like a comet. 'I Would Die 4 U' and 'Take Me With U' became the fourth and fifth US chart successes from the

The audiences loved Prince's new superstardom, but the critics found it hard to swallow. Before long the papers began to portray him as a mincing, narcissistic caricature of himself. Richard Grabel in the UK's *NME* said of Prince in 1985 that "He cannot see us. He sees only the great mirror in his mind's eye, which shows him only his big, royal self."

Around The World In A Day

With typically stylish ease, Prince had already completed a new album by the time the tour was over. Released in April 1985, it was naturally greeted with cool reviews by journalists who were waiting for *Purple Rain 2*, but it reached Number 1 on the *Billboard* chart and Number 5 in the UK, selling more than four million copies worldwide. Like his two preceding albums, *Around The World In A Day* took Prince further than ever from his black roots to a "psychedelic" sound (echoed in Doug Henders' vibrant cover art) with a Sixties pop-rock feel—more Sly Stone than James Brown.

Though voted Best International Artist at the BPI awards in London in 1985, Prince was mocked by the tabloids and reportedly vowed never to return. When he won again in 1993, his award was accepted by Cher on his behalf.

album. Prince was being showered with awards: the Minnesota Music Awards, the Grammys, a surprise appearance at the British Phonographic Institute in London, and an Oscar for best soundtrack at the Academy Awards. Meanwhile, in the UK the double A-side single '1999'/'Little Red Corvette' became Prince's biggest hit to date, followed into the Top 10 by 'Let's Go Crazy' in February 1985.

The Purple Prince

The singles garnered from the album were chirpy and positive pop melodies. 'Paisley Park' was about discovering the beauty in your own soul. 'Raspberry Beret' was an off-the-wall love song with a catchy chorus. 'America' was a conservative hymn to celebrate the future, and 'Pop Life' was a grinding rock song, which implored us to count our blessings because "everybody can't be on top".

The album reveals more of Prince's spiritual side with tracks like 'Temptation', in which God passes judgement on him. 'The Ladder', which was co-written by his father, also had a religious ambience, and the whole album was relatively lacking in sexual references. As a result of this seemingly uncommercial development, the press were on the one hand disappointed and on the other inspired. *The National Enquirer* published an interview with Chick Huntsberry—the huge bodyguard who had left Prince's employ as the result of a very expensive cocaine addiction—which portrayed Prince as a paranoid, workaholic religious maniac who had lost touch with real life. The headline ran: "The Real Prince. He's Trapped In A Secret Bizarre World Of Terror".

Paisley Park

Prince's warehouse recording studio was becoming inadequate. The purpose-built studio that replaced it

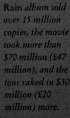

Above: the **Purple Rain** *album sold over 15 million copies, the movie took more than $70 million (£47 million), and the tour raked in $30 million (£20 million) more.*

Prince's royal throne—Paisley Park Studios in Chanhassen, near Minneapolis.

from the ashes of The Time, led by Paul Peterson, The Time's erstwhile keyboard player on the 1999 tour. Prince wrote, produced and played the instruments on an entire album of funky pop songs, for which "St Paul" was invited to provide vocals. The album, which featured the grandly orchestral track 'Nothing Compares 2 U', was released later in 1985 to little reaction from the public, and the band performed together on stage only once, at First Avenue in Minneapolis.

was in the middle of a Chanhassen cornfield off Highway 5, 20 miles south of Minneapolis. Prince christened it Paisley Park, the name of the new label on which the album was released. "Paisley Park is in everybody's heart," he said in a *Rolling Stone* interview. "It's not just something I have the keys to. In a life that was increasingly dominated by symbolism, the studio became Prince's spiritual centre, a place where he could immerse himself in work, regardless of the world outside.

The first Paisley Park protegés were The Family, a band who rose

Parade

Recorded in the summer of 1985, *Parade* did not surface until the following March. Accompanying Prince's second movie, *Under A Cherry Moon*, the album was presaged by 'Kiss' a jangly pop classic that went to Number 1 in the USA and Number 6 in the UK. 'Kiss' made it all seem so easy, with an irresistible beat, a funny and sexy falsetto vocal, and a groovy guitar sound all in one superb pop gem. *Parade* featured an augmented Revolution line-up with Miko Weaver joining Wendy

The Purple Prince

"Paisley Park is in everybody's heart. It's not just something I have the keys to."

Prince

on guitar, a horn section made up of Eric Leeds on saxophone and Atlanta Bliss (Matt Blistan) on trumpet, not to mention a 67-piece orchestra conducted by Clare Fischer. It was a big-sounding album and covered a lot of ground, from the biting rock of 'Anotherloverholenyohead' to the ambitious march of 'Christopher Tracy's Parade' and the stirring lament of 'Sometimes It Snows In April'.

The album also represented a drastic change of image for Prince, as the famous purple garments disappeared overnight to be replaced by fashionable linen suits and cut-off jackets with overemphasized buttons and pockets, all designed by

Marie France (who appears on the album, speaking in French).

The Parade tour

During the early part of 1986 Prince had played several one-off gigs and surprise appearances to introduce material from the *Parade* album, including a series of "hit and run" concerts announced by local radio stations shortly before the show. One such gig at the Warfield Theatre in San

The Grammys, BPI Awards, Academy Awards, American Music Awards, Minnesota Music Awards, ASCAP Awards...over the years Prince has accumulated more gold and silver than Liberace.

Francisco was announced only three hours before it started. The "new" Revolution, featuring the 11-piece line-up, débuted at First Avenue with a show that was radically different from the elaborate spectacle that had characterized the two previous tours. With Miko Weaver on guitar, Prince was able to perform more freely, and his dance routines became more integral to the show than ever before. As Robbi Millar wrote in his review of the show in *Sounds*: "Choreography doesn't seem an apt enough word." On August 12, 1986 Prince played the first of three sell-out London shows for which British fans had been waiting anxiously for years. He did not disappoint them. The critics were bowled over. The tabloid papers who had bestowed Prince with the nickname "Ponce" after several of the paparazzi had come to blows with

bodyguard Chick Huntsberry at the BPI awards were now overflowing with praise. The stage may have been bare, but Prince was alive and electric. More than just a return to the UK, this was a Second Coming, and since then British fans have welcomed his return appearances time and time again.

"I had a star in my eyes and a memory, forever, of heaven in my head."
Steve Sutherland reviewing
Prince at Wembley
(Melody Maker, August 1986)

Although the creative minds behind Prince's second movie were mostly unknowns, Warner Brothers were sufficiently impressed by the box-office appeal of *Purple Rain* to consider Prince a good risk. Initially

Opposite and above: *The end of the Revolution—Prince live in 1986. He cut his hair, he cut his jackets, and then he cut his band.*

The Purple Prince

pop video director Mary Lambert was contracted to direct *Under A Cherry Moon*, but when filming began on the French Riviera in September 1985, it soon became apparent that Prince intended to run the show himself.

In the movie, Prince takes the role of Christopher Tracy, a sharp lounge lizard who leaves America with his friend Tricky (played by Time sidekick Jerome Benton) in the hope of marrying a rich heiress. The result is a lightweight romantic comedy, shot in black and white for authentic 1930s atmosphere. Unfortunately, apart from attractive photography and good music, the film has little to offer. Prince's direction uses classic Hollywood techniques but lacks any recognizable style of its own, and the plot is mainly a distraction from the musical set pieces. The film was a box-office disappointment, which must have brought the versatile star down to earth somewhat.

Work in progress

As usual Prince was busy in the studio throughout the year. However, 1986 was a year of change for more than just his suits. March and April were spent hard at work with The Revolution on a planned album called *Dream Factory*. The sessions featured songs like

Overleaf: *On stage in 1986, laid-back as always.*

Francesca Annis with Prince in Under A Cherry Moon. *The film was a box-office disaster, earning only $3.2 million (£2.1 million) in its first week in the States.*

The movie opened in July 1986 in Sheridan, Wyoming following a nation-wide competition to "Win a première for your town!"

'Starfish And Coffee' and 'Can't Stop This Feeling I Got', which was to re-appear later in Prince's career, but many of the tracks were lost for ever. In a rare interview that year, Prince confessed to a Detroit DJ that he had more than 320 finished songs in his vaults.

The *Dream Factory* project was dropped when Prince made the sur-prise announcement in October that The Revolution had been disbanded. This was as much of a shock to the band as it was to the world. Prince had decided that he wanted to spend time working alone, and the result

69

was a huge burst of recording. To begin with, he wrote and produced an instrumental jazz fusion album for a band called Madhouse, a refreshing departure into a wildly complex and experimental kind of music. Using styles he had never tried before, Prince allowed his talent to be free of the constraints of stardom.

"I wouldn't mind if I just went broke, y'know, as long as I could still play."

Prince

From there, still on a creative high, he launched into more solo work, this time relishing the anonymity of a pseudonym. Prince became Camille, recording eight hot, funky dance tracks with highly sexual lyrics. However, the album—scheduled to reach the shops in January 1987—was never released and only 100 test pressings of the record were made. Six of the tracks, including 'Feel U Up' and 'Housequake', appeared later in his career, while 'Rockhard In A Funky Place' ended up on the equally ill-fated (and unnamed) *Black Album*. The eighth song, 'Rebirth Of The Soul' is still waiting to be reborn.

Prince had begun recording an album, to be called *Crystal Ball*, in LA in July while working with his protégées Sheila E (on her third album) and Jill Jones (on her début). With hindsight, it seems that he must have known, even before the Parade tour began, that it would be The Revolution's swan song. Tucked away in the basement of his new Chanhassen home, Prince worked tirelessly throughout the autumn on the ambitious triple album project, until he emerged with 21 newly recorded songs. However, Warner Brothers were not convinced by the idea of a three-record set, so *Crystal Ball* was whittled down to 16 songs on only two discs. The impressive, meandering 11-minute title track was cut, and the album became *Sign O' The Times*.

Chapter 4
The Greatest Show On Earth

Although neither his best-selling nor his most famous album, *Sign O' The Times* was in many ways Prince's crowning glory. For the first time, he consolidated the wide range of musical styles that had characterized his first eight albums. *Sign O' The Times* had everything that had made his spectacular career so exciting—the raunchiness of *Dirty Mind*, the rock of *Purple Rain*, and the studio perfection of *Parade*. The album was a true epic with something for everyone, but, like so many classics, it was largely underestimated at the time. As Prince's popularity in his home country dwindled, his record sales began to fall. The new double album sold only 3 million copies worldwide.

The Sign O' The Times tour

Supported by Madhouse, the Sign O' The Times tour began with two brief appearances at the Daily News and Melody clubs in Stockholm, before launching the tour proper with three nights at the 40,000-seat Istadion. The show opened each night with the hollow, funky title track and moved straight into the contrastingly uplifting 'Play In The Sunshine'. The set was brilliantly paced—dressed in peach and black, Prince danced frenetically to the pumping 'Housequake' and 'Hot Thing', slowed down for 'Slow Love' and 'Adore', and rocked out for 'I Could Never Take The Place Of Your Man' with its mesmerizing extended instrumental break. The show would come to an end with 'It's Gonna Be A Beautiful Night' (at the end of which Prince would gleefully shout "Confusion!", whereupon the band dissolved into chaotic noise) and 'The Cross', a gloriously spiritual anthem, which left the audience damp-eyed and exhausted.

The 34-night European tour was seen by 350,000 people, but few of them were British. Three concerts planned for Wembley Stadium were cancelled at short notice, with poor weather conditions given as an explanation. Indoor shows at Earls Court

Scottish singer Sheena Easton, who partnered Prince on 'U Got The Look'.

were hurriedly scheduled, but a licence was never granted. Two concerts at the Birmingham National Exhibition Centre (NEC), where Prince had rehearsed the show in April, were also cancelled. It was a tragic disappointment for British fans, many of whom tried to redeem their useless tickets for newly announced shows in Rotterdam.

Let's Work

The remainder of the year saw Prince as hard at work as ever, both on and off the stage. A second Madhouse album was completed (this time with percussion provided by Sheila E) as well as his next solo effort, which came to be known as the *Black Album*. In September he made more "hit and run" appearances, including the exclusive MTV Awards after-show party in LA, where he played a two-hour set featuring a cover of 'I Want To Take You Higher' by Sly Stone, who was in the audience.

The $10 million (£6.6 million) Paisley Park studio complex was

The Sign O'The Times stage set was transplanted to Paisley Park for the filming of the concert movie.

opened officially in 1987—although it had already been used by such varied and promising musicians as Taja Sevelle, Bonnie Raitt and World Party—and the world marvelled at its state-of-the-art design, which included an impressive 12,400-square foot recording room with impeccable acoustics.

Prince's first concert movie, *Sign O' The Times*, opened in October to excited reviews. Filmed partly at the Antwerp and Rotterdam shows in June, but mostly on the superb Paisley Park sound stage, it was hailed by UK magazine *Sky* as "the greatest concert movie ever made".

"The greatest concert movie ever made."

Sky magazine

The *Black Album*

One of Prince's most famous recordings, though never released, the *Black Album* has passed into popular music mythology. It is widely available as a bootleg, yet only a small quantity were pressed, of which just a hundred copies managed to find their way out of a plastics factory in Germany. The *Music Master Price Guide* estimates these original copies to be worth in the region of £1,000 ($1,500), adding that it "comes on to the market so rarely that its value has to be somewhat speculative".

Prince asked ticket-holders to wear peach or black to the Sign O' The Times gigs.

"I suddenly realized that we can die at any moment, and we'd be judged by the last thing we left behind."

Prince

The album was considered to be a low-key release: its cover would have been entirely black with only the catalogue number printed in peach on the spine. The music is hard funk and rap in the style of Prince's earlier Camille material. The best tracks are 'Le Grind', a smooth, sexy dance number; 'Superfunkycalifragisexy', a P-Funk style soul rant; '2 Nigs United 4 West Compton', a jazz-rock instrumental à la Madhouse; and 'When 2 R In Love', which was preserved for his next album. One of the most memorable of the tracks, opening side two, is 'Bob George', a sort of foul-mouthed fable in which Prince plays the part of a misogynist gangster rapper. The song turned up on the Lovesexy tour, and audiences loved the self-deprecating line: "Prince? That skinny muthafucker with the high voice?"

The reason for the album's sudden deletion has passed into legend. The Lovesexy tour programme explained rather obliquely that "Camille" had been overpowered by his negative side: "He had allowed the dark side

Camille *became* **Crystal Ball** *became* **Sign O' The Times,** *as Prince became a solo artist—not that he had ever been anything else.*

of him 2 create something evil," Prince wrote. He later revealed his reason in plainer English: "I was very angry a lot of the time back then," he said. "I suddenly realized that we can die at any moment, and we'd be judged by the last thing we left behind."

Lovesexy

With the inevitable press uproar, Prince's tenth album hit the shops on May 10, 1988. At least, it hit most of the shops; the cover art, which pictured Prince tastefully photographed in the nude by Jean Baptise Mondino, caused something of a stir among record retailers in the USA. Prince was perhaps a little naïve to expect any different. As Mavis Staples (of soul group the Staples Singers) told him in London later that year, "The people in the States aren't as broad-minded as the people here."

His disappointment is none the less understandable, for Prince believes that physical love is the ulti-mate expression of spiritual feeling and *Lovesexy* is a stylish attempt to clean the slate and turn his dirty-minded reputation into a spiritual rebirth. From the opening words ("The reason my voice is so clear is there's NO—SMACK—IN—MY—

The chilling Sign O' The Times *title track went Top 10 in the UK and US.*

Prince rocks out to the burning guitar solo from 'Sister' in the opening medley from the Lovesexy '88 tour.

BRAIN") Prince announces his new manifesto. The new era is based around songs such as 'Positivity' ("Positivity. Y—E—S. Have you had your plus sign 2-day?") and the title track, which the lyric sheet describes as: "The feeling U get when U fall in love not with a girl or a boy but with the heavens above."

In practice, the definition is a very personal one, but for the artist this was a cathartic work and he has

"He knew some things were wrong, that he was influencing young kids... In order to justify this he created this sort of new religion where it's OK, and God smiles on you."

Dez Dickerson

never looked back. *Lovesexy* reconciled Prince's sexual nature with his belief in God and the sacred gifts passed down by Him. Dez Dickerson summed up Prince's philosophy, albeit rather sceptically: "He knew

"Shut up, already. Damn!"

some things were wrong, that he was influencing young kids...In order to justify this he created this sort of new religion where it's OK, and God smiles on you."

The Lovesexy '88 tour

Leading the way as always, Prince was growing tired of his role as pop star. No longer trying to be all things to all people, in 1988 he matured into the

The Greatest Show On Earth

musician he is today, and only one all-singing, all-dancing world tour stood between Prince the pop star and Prince the Grandmaster of Dance.

With Miko Weaver on guitar, Levi Seacer on bass, Matt Fink and Boni Boyer on keyboards, raunchy vocalist Cat, brass from Eric Leeds and Atlanta Bliss and the ineffable Sheila E on drums, Prince set off on the most explosive world tour his fans had ever seen. Warming up with an exclusive show at Paisley Park in May while recording the video for 'Glam Slam', he unveiled the new circular stage that would make Lovesexy '88 the concert event of the year. Beginning in July in Paris, Prince played 32 European shows before nearly 500,000 ticket holders. It was a huge success.

Every bit of the stunning performance "in the round" was minutely choreographed. Prince entered in a gleaming Thunderbird and circum-navigated the stage on a hydraulic lift. With the audience all around him, his stagecraft was tested to the full, and he excelled himself (as always), as if it were the simplest thing in the world to hold the attention of 15,000 people for two hours.

The show began with a medley of raunchy oldies like 'Erotic City' and 'Jack U Off', pausing only during

The very mobile Cat, on the Lovesexy tour.

Arriving in London in '88 with Sheila E.

'Sister' as Prince stood in the spotlight, playing a spine-tingling solo with his custom-made Blue Angel guitar. Containing as many as 30 songs, the show was not only a collection of Prince's greatest hits, but also a spiritual metamorphosis, in which the star changed from the raunchy Prince of old, frolicking on a brass bed during 'Superfunkycalifragisexy', into the evangelistic preacher of 'God Is Alive'.

But, first and foremost, Lovesexy '88 was sheer, theatrical entertainment. Intimate moments, like his beautiful solo piano medley, collided head on with the stadium rock of the hit encores 'Purple Rain' and 'Alphabet St'. The lighting was a spectacle, the sound system a technical marvel (the entire PA system "flew" from the ceiling) and the band were one of Prince's most inexhaustible, Sheila E's nightly, blistering drum solo on a giant revolving riser being a highlight of the show.

Back in the UK

Lovesexy was Prince's biggest-selling album to date in the UK, and the first to reach Number 1. He paid back the fans who had been cheated of the 1987 shows by making a sensational seven sell-out appearances at the Wembley Arena, and two at the Birmingham NEC in July and August. In *Sounds* an effusive Robin Gibson said "the sheer exhilaration makes Prince more exciting and innovative than any other visiting megastar," while Paul Mathur reported in *Melody Maker*: "Any pop performance

The Greatest Show On Earth

that I'll ever see again will be just a dull scrawl on some muddy canvas." *Record Mirror* reviewer Nancy Culp called Lovesexy '88 simply "the greatest show on earth".

As before, the London shows were just one mighty celebration. As a special surprise, ex-Funkadelic vocalist George Clinton—who had only recently signed to Paisley Park—joined Prince on the last night at Wembley for a version of his crowd-pleasing 'Get Off Your Ass And Jam'. At a late-night party after the first show, the band performed another full two-hour show at the Camden Palace in north London. Mavis Staples joined in for a rendition of 'I'll Take You There' and Rolling Stone Ron Wood borrowed a guitar and climbed on stage while Prince did Mick Jagger impersonations for the crowd.

You know you're good, girl/I think you like to go down"—'Head' from the Dirty Mind LP.

"*Any pop performance that I'll ever see again will be just a dull scrawl on some muddy canvas.*"

Paul Mathur, Melody Maker

The American tour

The American leg of the tour, however, was a disappointment. Far from being a sell-out, the concerts actually cost the organizers more than they raised from ticket sales, thanks to the high cost of transporting the elaborate stage set. The tour opened at the Met Center in Prince's hometown, after which the band played yet another exclusive gig at Paisley Park for a lucky 600 people. The party did not end until almost daylight, when the Chanhassen authorities broke it up for disturbing the peace.

After 38 dates 600,000 Americans had seen the Lovesexy tour. Yet many members of the US press remained reluctant to praise Prince, despite his determination to pursue his own true vision. Michael Ostin, a Warner Brothers executive, had a reason for this: "As brilliant as he is, the audience had a hard time keeping up with him."

Batman

In the new year, amid rumours that Prince and his Paisley Park empire were in dire financial straits, a surprise

announcement was made that Prince and his manager Steve Fargnoli were to part company "amicably" after a decade together. With the unusual and ill-fated appointment of Albert Magnoli (the *Purple Rain* director whose only subsequent achievement had been the 1986 gymnastics turkey *American Anthem*) as his replacement, Prince made a successful eight-night tour of Japan before finishing work on his next album project at home.

"Didn't she tell U Lovesexy is the Glam of them all?" Prince with Cat on the '88 tour.

"Gentlemen, let's broaden our minds..."

The Greatest Show On Earth

On June 20, 1989, a little in advance of the movie, Prince released the album *Batman*. 'Batdance', a dark, hip-hop single that reached the top of the charts in the US and Number 2 in the UK, had already given the world a flavour of the album to come. It was a much-needed hit that instantly dispelled any rumours of financial ruin. With the help of the movie, which was breaking box-office records around the world, the album was a sure success, reaching Number 1 in the US, Britain and most of Europe and soon selling six million copies worldwide.

In fact Prince's *Batman* bears very little resemblance to the Tim Burton film, and although songs from the album do appear on the soundtrack, their inclusion is more by way of a crass Hollywood marketing ploy than any real rapport. Danny Elfman's incidental score and theme music suit Burton's quirky style far better. However, as an album in its own right, *Batman* is an intense dance music blitz with an evocative "story-line" of its own woven together by the disembodied voices of actors Michael Keaton, Kim Basinger and Jack Nicholson. New manager Albert Magnoli collaborated on videos of 'Batdance' and 'Partyman', the former acting as a visual counterpart to the entire album. In the short film, Prince became Gemini, a dual personality that comprised both Batman and The Joker in a struggle between good and evil. Likewise, as Damon Wise pointed out in *Sounds*, the album itself is "less a soundtrack than a psychotic two-act melodrama. Prince's *Batman* takes place in a one-seat auditorium. And Prince takes all the parts."

> *"Prince's Batman takes place in a one-seat auditorium. And Prince takes all the parts."*
>
> Damon Wise, *Sounds*

Graffiti Bridge

During 1989 Prince also spent time writing and recording with Jill Jones, Patti LaBelle, a re-formed Time and Dutch saxophonist Candy Dulpher (who, in typical Paisley Park style, was renamed Candy D). After announcing yet another massive world tour for the following year, he began work on a movie project. Initially Prince

worked with Kim Basinger to write and develop the plot of *Graffiti Bridge*, which Prince intended to be an unabashed sequel to the blockbusting *Purple Rain*. Unfortunately, after a disagreement with Basinger over royalties for the 'Scandalous Sex Suite' (a lengthy interpretation of the *Batman* album track, released in the States but not in Britain), the actress pulled out of her role as Prince's leading lady, to be replaced by Paisley Park recruit Ingrid Chavez. The idea for a sequel stemmed from a planned Broadway musical in which Prince had intended to co-star with Madonna.

Unlike *Purple Rain* and *Parade*, *Graffiti Bridge* was a genuine soundtrack album, featuring performances by The Time ('Release It', 'Love Machine', 'Shake!', 'The Latest Fashion') and the Jacksonesque vocals of boy wonder Tevin Campbell (singing 'Round And Round' which became a successful single in its own right). The album was an outright statement of Prince's vision. Although it lacked any obvious classic single material, it was dotted with tracks that had been part of Prince's vast repertoire for years, and along with his new, unashamedly funky material, the older tracks like 'Joy In Repetition' finally came into their own.

Graffiti Bridge was dominated by the kind of hard dance-funk that Prince had normally reserved for artists other than himself. His last few albums had played safe, his experimental side flourishing only in the relative anonymity of songwriting. This new album was an extremely lengthy collection (17 tracks), taking

Left to right: *Boni Boyer, Sheila E and Cat at Wembley Arena in London, July 1988.*

in everything from the solid rock of 'Thieves In The Temple' to the slow, jazzy blues of 'Melody Cool' (featuring Mavis Staples), and the heartwarming, spiritual carol of 'Still Would Stand All Time'. Critics did not react well to the album, but that was old news. It took Prince to Number 1 in the UK album charts for the third time in three years—the first black artist to achieve this.

Box-office flop

The movie of *Graffiti Bridge* was never released on the UK cinema circuit. In the United States it opened in November 1990, taking almost $4 million (£2.6 million) in the first

The Greatest Show On Earth

"I'm not looking to be Francis Ford Coppola. I see this more like those 1950s rock 'n' roll movies."
Prince

Prince displays his moody Graffiti Bridge persona.

week. However, after the promising opening, the box-office revenue soon dwindled into an embarrassing trickle and the movie was finally withdrawn from cinemas after only two weeks.

The reviews had been terrible, not to say cruel. Prince complained that critics had expected too much from the film. "I'm not looking to be Francis Ford Coppola," he reasoned. "I see this more like those 1950s rock 'n' roll movies." However, after the financial bashing, Warners were extremely wary of the movie's potential losses, and it was only ever made available in Britain on video. Prince's career as a movie star seemed to be finally over.

Chapter 5

The Sign Of A Star

The new decade witnessed a transformation in Prince's career. No longer pandering to the press or lowering himself to the level of daytime pop radio, he allowed his experimental side—his true musical soul—to express itself. While much of his work in the 1990s has not been obviously commercial, at the same time he has been pushing at the boundaries of commercial acceptability.

The Nude tour
Taking their name from a song on *Graffiti Bridge*,

Prince unveiled a new backing band, the New Power Generation. With a considerable contribution from the heavyweight operatic vocalist Rosie Gaines, the band featured Levi Seacer on bass, Michael Bland on drums, Miko Weaver on guitar and Matt Fink on keys, plus three rappers and dancers called the Game Boyz, who had previously appeared as extras in *Purple Rain*.

The Nude tour opened with two nights in Rotterdam, followed by a marathon 49 dates around Europe over three months and then on to Japan. The whole thing was different to any of the previous touring shows. The stage set was glitzy yet not overblown, and the set list was dynamic, but without any theme. The songs were mainly upbeat hits—it was a mercilessly big, black dance show with Prince's best-known dancefloor tracks like 'Housequake', 'Alphabet St' and 'Partyman' getting the crowd on their feet. He also paid tribute to other songwriters with a series of cover versions, including a show-stopping take on the Aretha Franklin hit 'Respect'.

A record-breaking run of 16 gigs at Wembley Arena in London sold nearly 200,000 tickets, and Prince played 21 dates in Britain overall, as well as making his first appearance in Ireland at the Pairc U Chaiomh in Cork. Undoubtedly it was this leg of the tour that provided the most thrilling moments. Prince was on a high, with *Graffiti Bridge* newly released and 'Thieves In The Temple' rocketing into the Top 10. The tour swept through London, Birmingham and Manchester like a whirlwind, proving to the fans—if not always to the ever-doubting press—that Prince was a new breed of showman who was more fresh and inspiring after 12 albums than he had been after the first.

Pandemonium

A few days after the Nude tour moved on, The Time were in London for a few low-key concerts in support of their unexpected fourth album, *Pandemonium*. The

Opposite page:
The New Power Generation.

The Nude tour coincided with the release of Prince's ambitious twelfth album, Graffiti Bridge.

Tracks from **Diamonds And Pearls** *were previewed at the Rock in Rio festival in Brazil (right and opposite page), in January 1991. MTV filmed the entire event, but Prince's set was never transmitted, because he bought the rights himself.*

album was to become their biggest-selling and most successful to date, while 'Jerk Out' was their biggest hit single, reaching the *Billboard* Number 18. Although, as ever, songwriting credits can be traced back to the mysterious Prince alter-ego Jamie Starr, the sleeve-notes name the composers as Time members Morris Day, Jimmy Jam, Terry Lewis and Monte Moir. *Pandemonium* is an extension of frontman Morris Day's on-stage caricatured personality. It is a braggish, masculine album about girls, cars and hard cash, but all delivered in an irresistibly uptempo high-camp manner. However, the reunion of The Time was unlikely to continue much longer. Jam and Lewis were by now a great success in their own right, having recently put Janet Jackson into the charts with the hit 'What Have You Done For Me Lately?'

Songwriter to the stars

The rest of 1990 was spent in rehearsal with the New Power Generation, while Prince worked tirelessly on songs for his next album. In December he worked with Martika on several tracks for her album *Martika's Kitchen*. This was only one of many songwriting collaborations. Since Prince had achieved stardom, he had been in constant demand as a hitmaking songwriter. After donating 'Manic Monday' to the Bangles, he helped to make a star of Sheena Easton with 'Sugar Walls', made a dream partnership with Madonna in 1989 with 'Love Song' on her *Like A Prayer* album, and briefly revived Kid Creole's struggling career with 'The Sex Of It' in 1990.

One song, 'Glam Slam', from the *Lovesexy* album, was donated to his friend Gilbert Davison—not to be recorded, but the title to be

used as the name of a new nightclub in downtown Minneapolis. Glam Slam, like First Avenue, has become a Mecca for Prince fans, and carries the full Paisley Park seal of approval. The New Power Generation first appeared there in early 1991, and for a while Davison acted as Prince's manager, replacing movie director Albert Magnoli, before Prince decided to take on the job himself.

In 1990 a cover version of a virtually unknown Prince song, 'Nothing Compares 2 U', was released as a single by Sinead O'Connor, accompanied by a striking video in which the singer was said to have been brought to tears in front of the camera. The single was a massive success, staying at the UK Number 1 spot for five weeks. However, Sinead O'Connor was clearly not destined to become another one of Prince's malleable protegées. As a young and outspoken Irish feminist her opinions clashed violently with Prince's, and their first meeting in Minneapolis was also their last. O'Connor later related the story of an embarrassing row between the two, at the end of which Prince

refused to talk to her, or even to call her a taxi.

'Gett Off'

'Gett Off' was more than ever a sign of Prince's new hardcore dance direction, making the UK Number 4. The single was followed by a five-song video collection, which itself made Number 1 on *Billboard*'s video sales chart. Every line simmered with open sexuality, with throatily spoken lines like: "Bring your big ass round and let me work on that zipper, baby..." For a hit single it was daringly crude, but Prince was barely scratching the surface. His promotional tour was completed with a performance of 'Gett Off' on the MTV Video Music Awards in LA. This unusual level of self-exposure unarguably boosted Prince's appeal and 'Cream', his next

With Rosie Gaines and the rest of the New Power Generation during the Diamonds and Pearls world tour in 1992.

97

newest album in October 1991. *Diamonds And Pearls* was well received by critics for its combination of uncompromising funk and classy, jazzy soul. In America, four of the album tracks became Top 30 hits: the very traditional ballad 'Diamonds And Pearls', the pounding rock single 'Thunder', the notorious 'Gett Off' and the bouncy pop hit 'Cream'. Although 'Gett Off' and 'Push' were stripped-down house and rap numbers, the album as a whole was intentionally less "digital" than *Batman*. The influence of NPG member Rosie Gaines provided soulful, Sixties harmonizing, as well as some thick, treacly keyboard sounds. There was a gospel feel to much of the album, backed up by bold R&B brass. As Prince told Scott Poulson-Bryant of *Spin*: "Everybody else went out and got drum machines and computers, so I threw mine away." Although this is clearly not entirely true, *Diamonds And Pearls* did prove Prince to be at the leading edge of dance music, combining his well-heeled flair with the street-sound of the Nineties. The album went to the

single, swiftly went to Number 1 on the *Billboard* chart, his biggest success since 'Batdance' and his fifth Number 1 single in the US.

Diamonds And Pearls

After a season of postponements, Warner Brothers released Prince's

Rosie Gaines, the soulful chanteuse of the New Power Generation.

musicians while a fast-talking music-biz manager chattered in the background. The song provoked Steve Fargnoli to file a $5 million (£3.3 million) law suit against Paisley Park for defamation of character. The case was later settled out of court.

The next world tour

Prince was already itching to return to the road again in early 1992. At Glam Slam in January he previewed another set list bristling with newly rehearsed material. The band had recorded as many as 30 new songs in three months at Paisley Park, while Prince had donated "spare" songs to rapper Monie Love and a Dutch band called Lois Lane, who had supported some of the Nude dates.

The New Power Generation had grown: a five-piece horn section now filled the stage and gave the band a classic Stax soul sound. Their first appearance outside Minneapolis was in Tokyo, as another 50-date world tour commenced with two gigs at the giant 50,000-seat Dome. Although many fans had expected to see a basic rock 'n' roll show, the Diamonds and

top of the US chart and to Number 2 in Britain, selling in excess of five million copies worldwide.

One song caused more controversy than any other, because Prince's ex-manager was convinced that it was an attempt to mimic and humiliate him. Rapper Tony M made a potent contribution to the album, and on 'Jughead' he gave advice to young

"I don't try to do anything to shock people or to take money—that would make me a hooker."
—Prince

"A spellbinding display of Prince's absolute musical genius."

Herald-Sun

Pearls tour was in fact his most sumptuous production to date. The stage was overhung by glittering stars and laced with platforms, steps and ramps. Once again, Prince took the stage dramatically. As a blazing lighting rig (in the shape of his trademark male/female symbol) hovered overhead, he appeared before the audience from a large space capsule. Prince and his dancers (including another newcomer, Egyptian ballerina Mayte Garcia) moved with seemingly inexhaustible energy, leaving the audience more breathless than the performers. To slow down the pace between frantic numbers like '1999' and 'Cream', Rosie Gaines took centre stage for magnificent renditions of 'Chain Of Fools' and 'Dr Feelgood'. Prince closed the show with a punchy new rap track called 'My Name Is Prince' and a dash through Sheila E's 'A Love Bizarre' into the rap rave 'Push'.

The New Power Generation crossed the Pacific for Prince's first-ever Australian dates, playing 14 gigs to a total of 200,000 fans. The fever of the press was a match even for the

Princemania of the '86 UK tour. The *Herald-Sun* called the show "a spell-binding display of Prince's absolute musical genius". After the Brisbane gigs, one journalist described the Diamonds and Pearls tour as "the hottest act on the planet".

Moving on to Europe, the tour eventually arrived in London in June for a run of eight shows at Earls Court, then went on to Manchester and Glasgow for stadium gigs before concluding the three-month tour

"Makes Michael Jackson look nailed to the floor."
Denver Post

"Like all truly great artists, Prince is sick."—Melody Maker

in France. For the ecstatic fans it was hard to believe that Prince could remain so prolific and yet still spend so much time on the road. More incredible still, he would be back on tour only a year later.

In September Warner Brothers announced that Prince's various contracts had been renegotiated. Referring only to publishing rights and recording fees (but not to video royalties, tours or movies) the funding that was promised to Paisley Park amounted to $100 million (£67 million). Since that time there have been very few rumours of financial problems for the Minneapolis star.

☿

Prince and the New Power Generation released the follow-up to *Diamonds And Pearls* in October 1992. Titled simply and mysteriously ☿, the album featured almost 75 minutes of music tied loosely together by a "rock soap opera" theme. The first single from the album, 'Sexy MF', was an outrageous choice and gained airplay only because a specially recorded "radio-friendly" version

"You know, if you don't give me the real story, I'll have to make one up on my own..." Kirstie Alley plays the part of a probing reporter between tracks on Prince's 1992 album.

was released. The profane lyrics held back sales in America, but in the UK it reached Number 5 in the charts.

Toying with techno sounds and bizarre samples again, the album meandered between the traditional full-band rock of 'The Continental' and the raw, basic, egocentric rap of 'My Name Is Prince'. This song more than any other gave easy copy to journalists eager to pick apart Prince's unpredictable style. The song is delivered as a true hip-hop attack, full of poker-faced braggadocio ("In the beginning God made the sea, but on

the seventh day he made me") and black power ("I put my foot in the ass of Jim Crow, 12 inches of non-stop sole"). Consequently, critics called the album "bombastic" and "indulgent", while the more generous thought of it as a puzzle. Even within Paisley Park, the significance of the title was a mystery. A series of videos for the songs on the album was promised, with the true meaning to be revealed in the final film, but to date no such explanation has appeared. The theme of the album concerns Prince's affair with an eastern princess, but the songs are broken up by clips of a telephone conversation, which seems somehow to undermine the thread. The album closes with the (possibly semi-autobiographical) 'Sacrifice Of Victor', which extols the virtues of education. In the year to come, this song would be interpreted by more than one journalist as the key to the most bizarre and public mystery of Prince's career.

The first leg of the 1993 tour took in ten cities across the USA, playing multiple dates in small, intimate venues. Not surprisingly, tickets were

like gold dust—a show at Radio City Music Hall in New York sold out in nine minutes, and the venue for the opening gig in Fort Lauderdale, Florida, claimed to have shaved 60 seconds off that record. Performing most of the tracks from the ♀ album,

No pictures, please. Oh, all right then, just the one.

from the rockin' '7' to the romantic 'Blue Light', Prince played a two-hour set in a variety of costumes. For the first time in seven years the star was seen in the lacy, Edwardian-style coat that earmarked the *Purple Rain* years, perhaps a sign that in his determination to always move forwards, Prince is never afraid to look back.

Prince to retire?

April 27, 1993. A press release from Paisley Park: "Prince announced today that after releasing 15 albums in 15 years, he is turning his creative talents to alternative media—including live theater, interactive media, nightclubs and motion pictures... The move was prompted by Prince's growing need to explore less conventional approaches to music and media in order to keep up with escalating advances in technology.

The Sign Of A Star

'The future of the entertainment business not only embraces innovation but demands it,' said Gilbert Davison, president of Paisley Park enterprises, about Prince's decision."

After this announcement, Prince grabbed further press coverage with the most unaccountable move in his history. Turning 35 on June 7, 1993, he proclaimed that he was changing his name to ♀, the symbol that is usually considered to be a meaningless corruption of the male and female symbols. In Britain, *NME* reported the news with the headline: "My Name Is ♀ ... And I Am Bonkers!", which summed up public opinion fairly well. Even the rare fans who did not consider the move to be a demand for attention struggled to find even a glimmer of reason behind it. Official statements from the record company now refer to him as "our superstar, formerly known as Prince".

One journalist, basing his interpretation on words from 'The Sacrifice Of Victor', took the symbol to mean that we should now call Prince by that name. The rumour spread rapidly across Europe, despite an official

"Prince announced today that after releasing 15 albums in 15 years, he is turning his creative talents to alternative media."

Press release

press release to the contrary, and "Victor" became the star's new name for a lot of misinformed readers.

The last NPG tour
The British shows of the European tour were both thrilling and momentous. With the thought of "the last-ever New Power Generation tour" hanging in the air, fans flocked to see Prince in Birmingham, Edinburgh, Sheffield and London in July and August. Premiering new material like 'Come', 'Peach' and 'Pope', the NPG went out with a bang not a whimper. Although the set list was separated broadly into two halves (first a selection of new material and then a collection of audience favourites) the European tour had a special set each night. Borrowing an idea from David

"*The diminutive purple one gave pretty close to maximum bang for the buck. Sexy, strong, versatile: there's no reason for his reign to end.*"—Boston Globe, *March 1993*

Opposite page: *Prince's latest protégée, Carmen Elektra, released her self-titled début album on Paisley Park Records in 1993.*

Bowie's 1990 world tour, fans were given a telephone number so that they could call in their favourite Prince songs, and the band tried their best to play them all.

The after-show party at London's Forum (formerly the Town and Country Club) on July 31 was packed with delighted gig-goers who had been to the 72,000-capacity Wembley Stadium show that evening. Prince played a whole set of covers by his own favourite artists, including a superb, bluesy version of the Rolling Stones' 'Honky Tonk Women'.

The final gig of the tour, at Wembley Arena on September 7, was accompanied by two extraordinary events. First, in the morning, Prince went to Broadcasting House, the home of BBC Radio, to perform in a splendid disused concert hall, which had not seen a rock music performance since Jimi Hendrix took the stage there in 1968. The gig was transmitted live on Simon Bates's morning show on Radio One. Later, after the Wembley performance was over, the band and many of the audience moved on to King's Cross and the hideaway venue Bagley's Warehouse. "The Dawn" was one of a series of "raves" on the European tour, and the small club was soon heaving with Prince's admirers, who had snapped up the strictly limited tickets.

Not only did Prince and the band play another full set, but they also sent out a camera crew to interview ravers in the audience. The resulting film from the exclusive warehouse gig was turned into a 45-minute film entitled "The Sacrifice of Victor", which was premiéred on MTV in January 1994. Although the concert movie features Prince on stage throughout, the spotlight is on the whole of the Paisley Park gang, including Mavis Staples, the Steeles and the New Power Generation. Prince takes the microphone only

"One of his
microphones was
a hilariously
phallic pistol, the
poured-on outfits
were cockadoodle
delirious and the
singer has the kind
of moves Barry
White can only
talk about."—
Washington Post,
March 15, 1993

for 'Peach' and for a brief blast of
'Jailhouse Rock'.

Appetite for production
In September '93, two long-awaited
compilation albums (*The Hits* and
The Hits 2) were released, and both
rocketed straight into the UK Top
10. For Prince, becoming the elusive

Prince sporting his latest 'Typhoon' hairstyle.

♀ was a typically scatty decision, both knowingly bizarre and wittily cryptic. It was the end of an era, and undoubtedly the beginning of a new one.

Having worked on arrangements of 13 of his songs for the respected Joffrey Ballet's latest show, Prince has already proved that he is keen to experiment. Whether his next project

be a ballet, a movie, a theme park or a video game, one thing is certain—whatever Prince works on, he always does it in style.

Warner Brothers are doubtless set to release old Prince songs for decades to come (and they have some brilliant work to choose from, like the unreleased classics 'Neon Telephone' and 'Crystal Ball'). An album of recent numbers cannot be ruled out; Prince is said to be working well as part of a rock five-piece featuring Paisley Park newcomers, the result of which could be a collection of unbridled rock 'n' roll songs with the newly patented single-word titles. A new spin-off record label, NPG Records, may soon be launched, but Prince's Paisley Park Records was laid to rest in early 1994.

Since his teenage days when he was jamming in Champagne with his friends, Prince's creativity has never ceased. His appetite for work—be it as singer, musician, producer or writer—has been unequalled and whatever his plans may be for the future, we can be sure that retirement is definitely not one of them.

Since 'Little Red Corvette' in 1983, Prince has had at least one entry in the US Top 10 every year.

113

Chronology

1958			Ruffalo and manager		(Number 9)
June 7	Born Prince Roger Nelson, Minneapolis, Minnesota, USA		Steve Fargnoli	Dec	First appearance on MTV boosts Triple Threat tour
1974	Forms first band, Grand Central, with André Anderson	Aug	Release of first US chart hit, 'I Wanna Be Your Lover'		
		Dec	Début UK single 'I Wanna Be Your Lover'	**1983** Feb	First US Top 10 single 'Little Red Corvette'
1976					
Sept	Signs management deal with American Artists Inc	**1980** Jan	Release of *Prince*	**1984** May	First US Number 1 single 'When Doves Cry' released: becomes best-selling single of the year
1977		Oct	Release of *Dirty Mind*		
June 25	Signs up with Warner Brothers Records	Winter	First US tour begins		
		1981		June	'When Doves Cry' reaches UK Number 4. Release of album *Purple Rain*
1978		May	First European tour		
April 7	Début album *For You* released	Oct	Release of *Controversy*	July	Release of movie *Purple Rain*
June	Début single 'Soft And Wet' released	Nov	Controversy tour begins in US	Nov	Purple Rain tour begins
1979		**1982**			
Summer	Signs with management team Cavallo &	Nov	First US Top 10 album, *1999*	**1985**	Purchases a property

Chronology

1987

March   *Sign O' The Times* released

Summer   Sign O' The Times tour begins

Oct   *Sign O' The Times* film opens

1988

May   *Lovesexy* released

July   Lovesexy '88 tour begins

1989   Manager Steve Fargnoli replaced by Albert Magnoli

June   *Batman* album released

1990

Jan   Sinead O'Connor's hit single 'Nothing Compares 2 U' released

June   The Nude tour begins

July   *Graffiti Bridge* released

Nov   *Graffiti Bridge* film opens

1991

Oct   *Diamonds And Pearls* released: Steve Fargnoli files a lawsuit for 'Jughead'

1992

Spring   Diamonds and Pearls tour begins, including first ever dates in Australia

Sept   New deal with Warner is worth $100 million (£67 million).

Oct   ♀ album released

1993

April   Prince announces "retirement" from studio recording.

June   Prince turns 35 and changes his name to ♀ .

Summer   Prince appears with New Power Generation for the last time in Europe.

Sept   *Hits 1* and *Hits 2* released

in Minnesota, which becomes known as Paisley Park

April   Release of *Around The World In A Day*

1986

March   Release of *Parade*

Spring   Parade tour begins

July   *Under A Cherry Moon* film opens

Oct   The Revolution is disbanded

PRINCE DISCOGRAPHY

Italics indicate first release date: singles chart positions indicate highest position ever reached by that track as an A-side.

ALBUMS

For You
April 1978
Charts: UK-, US 163
US: Warner 3150-2

Prince
January 1980
Charts: UK-, US 22
UK:WEA 256772-2
US: Warner 3366-2

Dirty Mind
October 1980
Charts: UK-, US 45
UK: Warner 256862
US: Warner 3478-2

Controversy
October 1981
Charts: UK-,US 21
UK: Warner 256950
US: Warner 3601-2

1999 (Full Version)

November 1983
Charts: UK 30, US 9
UK: Warner 923720-2
US: Warner 23720-2

Purple Rain
July 1984
Charts: UK 7, US 1
UK: Warner 925110-2
US: Warner 25110-2

Around The World In A Day
April 1985
Charts: UK 5, US 1
UK: Paisley Park 925286-2
US: Warner 25286-2

Parade
March 1986
Charts: UK 4, US 3
UK: Warner 925395-2
US: Warner 25395-2

Sign O' The Times
March 1987
Charts: UK 4, US 6
UK: Warner 925577-2
US: Warner 25577-2

Lovesexy
May 1988

Charts: UK 1, US 11
UK: WEA WX-164CD
US: Warner 25720-2

Batman
June 1989
Charts: UK 1, US 1
UK: WEA 925936-2
US: Warner 25936-2

Graffiti Bridge
July 1990
Charts: UK 1, US 6
UK: WEA 7599-27493-2
US: Warner 27493-2

Diamonds And Pearls
October 1991
Charts: UK 2, US 1
UK: Warner 7599-25379-2
US: Warner 25379-2

Symbol
October 1992
UK: Paisley Park 9362-450372
US: Warner 45037-2

The Hits Vol. 1
September 1993
US:Warner 45431

DISCOGRAPHY

The Hits Vol. 2
September 1993
US: Warner 45435

The Hits (3 disc boxed set)
September 1993
US: Warner 45440

SINGLES
Soft And Wet
June 1978
Charts: UK-, US 92

Just As Long As We're Together
November 1978
Charts: UK NR, US-

I Wanna Be Your Lover
December 1979
Charts: UK 41, US-

Why You Wanna Treat Me So Bad
January 1980
Charts: UK NR, US-

Sexy Dancer
April 1980
Charts: UK-, US NR

Uptown
September 1980
Charts: UK NR, US-

Dirty Mind
November 1980

Charts: UK NR, US-

Do It All Night
March 1981
Charts: UK-, US NR

Gotta Stop (Messin' About)
May 1981
Charts: UK-, US NR

Controversy
September 1981
Charts: UK2, US 70

Let's Work
April 1982
Charts: UK-, US-

Do Me Baby
July 1982
UK NR, US-

1999
September 1982
Charts: UK 25, US 44

Little Red Corvette
February 1983
Charts: UK 35, US 6

Delirious
August 1983
Charts: UK NR, US 8

Let's Pretend We're Married

November 1983
Charts: UK NR, US 52

When Doves Cry
June 1984
Charts: UK 4, US 1

Purple Rain
September 1984
Charts: UK 8, US 2

I Would Die 4 U
November 1984
Charts: UK 58, US 8

Let's Go Crazy
February 1985
Charts: UK 7, US 1

Paisley Park
May 1985
Charts: UK 18, US NR

Raspberry Beret
July 1985
Charts: UK 25, US 2

Pop Life
October 1985
Charts: UK 60, US 7

America
October 1985
Charts: UK NR, US 46

DISCOGRAPHY

Kiss
February 1986
Charts: UK 6, US 1

Mountains
June 1986
Charts: UK 45, US 23

Girls And Boys
August 1986
Charts: UK 11, US NR

Anotherloverholenyohead
October 1986
Charts: UK 36, US 63

Sign O' The Times
March 1987
Charts: UK 10, US 3

If I Was Your Girlfriend
June 1987
Charts: UK20, US 67

U Got The Look
July 1987
Charts: UK 11,US 2

I Could Never Take The Place Of
Your Man
November 1987
Charts: UK 29, US 10

Alphabet St
April 1988

Charts: UK 9, US 10

Glam Slam
July 1988
Charts: UK 29, US-

I Wish U Heaven
October 1988
Charts: UK 24, US-

Batdance
June 1989
Charts: UK 2, US 1

Partyman
July 1989
Charts: UK 14, US 18

The Arms Of Orion
October 1989
Charts: UK 27, US 32

Scandalous (Sex Suite)
November 1989
Charts: UK NR, US-

Thieves In The Temple
July 1990
Charts: UK 7, US 6

New Power Generation
November 1990
Charts UK 26, US NR

Gett Off

August 1991
Charts: UK 4, US 21

Cream
September 1991
Charts: UK 15, US 1

Diamonds And Pearls
November 1991
Charts: UK 25, US 3

Money Don't Matter 2 Night
March 1992
Charts: UK 19, US 23

Thunder
June 1992
Charts: UK 30, US NR

Sexy MF
July 1992
Charts: UK 4, US 66

My Name Is Prince
September 1992
Charts: UK 7, US 36

7
November 1992
Charts: UK 27, US-

The Morning Papers
March 1993
UK-, US-

INDEX

Index